Peter Cottontail
IS ON HIS WAY

By Andrea Posner
Illustrated by Linda Karl and Christopher Nowell

A GOLDEN BOOK • NEW YORK

Golden Books Publishing Company, Inc., New York, New York 10106

Library of Congress Catalog Card Number: 99-67532 ISBN: 0-307-99506-2 A MM First Edition 2000

We'd be happy to answer your questions and hear your comments. Please call us toll free at 1-888-READ-2-ME (1-888-732-3263). Hours: 8 AM–8 PM EST, weekdays. US and Canada only.

It was the day before Easter in April Valley, and Colonel Wellington B. Bunny was deciding who should replace him as Chief Easter Bunny.

The Chief Easter Bunny is in charge of carving chocolates, sewing bonnets, and, of course, decorating and delivering Easter eggs.

"Peter Cottontail is a likely candidate," he
said to himself. "I know he's not perfect, but
he reminds me of me when I was his age."

Later that day, Colonel Bunny presented Peter Cottontail with his official egg basket.

"Carry it with pride," he told the happy rabbit. But just as the Colonel was about to declare Peter the new Chief Easter Bunny, nasty Irontail arrived.

"According to the constitution of April Valley," Irontail announced, "the Chief Easter Bunny shall be the one who delivers the most eggs."

Irontail then challenged Peter to an egg delivering contest that would take place the very next day.

"I'm not afraid of Irontail," Peter told the Colonel confidently.

Peter was so sure he was going to win that he threw a big party. He stayed up very late that night. Before he went to bed, he told his rooster alarm to wake him at 5:30 the next morning.

As soon as Peter was asleep, Irontail snuck into his house and fed magic bubblegum to the rooster. The next morning the rooster couldn't cock-a-doodle-doo! Peter slept on and on all through Easter day.

That same morning Irontail set out to deliver his
Easter eggs. Nobody wanted an egg from such a
nasty bunny. Though he tried all day long, he was able
to give away only one egg.

But since Peter didn't deliver any eggs at all, Irontail
won the contest.

Peter Cottontail knew that he had let everybody down. He left April Valley promising to make it up to them, somehow. After walking for days and days, Peter found himself in the Garden of Surprises with Seymour Sassafrass.

Peter told Mr. Sassafrass what had happened. "And there isn't anything I can do about it because Easter is over," Peter added.

Mr. Sassafrass had just the thing to help. "It's a Yestermorrow Mobile," he explained to Peter. "It can transport you into yesterday or tomorrow."

Antoine the pilot would take Peter back to Easter so he could deliver his eggs and win the contest!

But not everything went as planned. Irontail discovered what Peter was up to and sent his spider to fiddle with the wires of the Yestermorrow Mobile. Instead of heading to Easter, Antoine and Peter landed right in the middle of Mother's Day.

Peter tried his best, but no one wanted painted eggs on Mother's Day.

Next they flew into a Fourth of July celebration.
"No one is going to want Easter eggs on the Fourth
of July either," Peter said sadly.

"Easter eggs no, but Fourth of July eggs, maybe.
You just have to improvise," suggested Antoine.

Peter found costumes and paint and tried giving out
eggs as the Independence Day Bunny. But still no one
wanted them.

Peter had the same bad luck on

Halloween,

Thanksgiving,

*and
Christmas.*

The next stop was Valentine's Day. Peter painted a
whole basket of red and pink Valentine eggs. Surely,
someone would want these beautiful eggs. But when
Peter wasn't looking, Irontail found the eggs and put
an evil spell on them. He turned them green—inside
and out!

No one at the Valentine's Day party wanted Peter's
green eggs. He hopped back into the Yestermorrow
Mobile, more upset than ever.

Before long Peter made another crash landing. This time he found himself in the middle of St. Patrick's Day.

Everywhere Peter looked, he saw green. He stood on a sidewalk offering free green eggs to anyone who wanted them.

Peter's shamrock eggs were the hit of the St. Patrick's Day parade. He gave away all of his eggs and finally won the contest.

Back in April Valley, Colonel Bunny congratulated Peter. "You have shown great ingenuity. Therefore, you have won the right to be the official Chief Easter Bunny," he said.

Easter morning, everyone cheered as Peter delivered bonnets, jelly beans, chocolates, and, of course, Easter eggs to all the children in the world.